IMOGENE TRIPP'S HISTORICAL TIDBITS

"FOUR SCORE AND SEVEN YEARS AGO" are the first words of Abraham Lincoln's Gettysburg Address. Given during the Civil War to dedicate a battlefield and define the war as a struggle for the equality of all Americans, it is one of the most famous speeches in our history. Is it any wonder these were Imogene's first words, too?

THE OREGON TRAIL—Pioneers in covered wagons followed this route west in the mid-1800s across hot, empty deserts and over rugged, snow-capped mountains on their way to settle territories on the Pacific coast.

DR. MARTIN LUTHER KING, JR.—In one of his sermons, this great civil rights leader talked about the role of history in people's lives. "We are not makers of history," he said. "We are made by history."

DAVY CROCKETT—In 1835, this frontiersman joined the fight to free Texas, which was not part of the United States at that time, from Mexico. He and about two hundred other men hunkered down inside a mission compound called the Alamo and tried to make a stand. Sadly, they were outnumbered by the Mexicans. Davy knew they needed reinforcements. When he realized none were on the way, legend claims he said, "Ain't nobody comin'." Thirteen days later, all the men at the Alamo, including Davy, were killed.

WILLIAM MORRIS—More than a hundred years ago, this English writer and craftsman tried to encourage people to save historic sites, saying, "Old buildings do not belong to us; they belonged to our forefathers, and they will belong to our descendants."

JOHN PAUL JONES—During the Revolutionary War, this naval officer found himself in a fierce sea battle against a British ship. Even as his own ship began to sink, Jones refused to surrender. "I have not yet begun to fight!" he cried. And fight he did, winning the battle and becoming a hero.

PAUL REVERE went down in history for his famous midnight ride, which marked the beginning of the American Revolution. On the night of April 18, 1775, he galloped from Boston to Lexington, Massachusetts, warning American colonists that British troops were on their way. Legend has it that as he rode, he shouted, "The British are coming! The British are coming!"

To April and Cyndi, those
passionate, confident, real-life
Imogenes. You go, girls!
—C.F.

For Tanya
—N.C.

Visit us on the Web! randomhouse.com/kids
Educators and librarians, for a variety of teaching tools,
visit us at RHTeachersLibrarians.com

The Library of Congress has cataloged the hardcover edition of this work as follows:
Fleming, Candace.
Imogene's last stand / Candace Fleming ; illustrated by Nancy
Carpenter. — 1st ed.   p. cm.
Summary: Enamored of history, young Imogene Tripp tries to save her town's historical
society from being demolished in order to build a shoelace factory.
ISBN 978-0-375-83607-7 (trade)— ISBN 978-0-375-93607-4 (glb) —
ISBN 978-0-375-98285-9 (ebook)
[1. Self-reliance—Fiction. 2. United States—History—Fiction.]
I. Carpenter, Nancy, ill. II. Title.
PZ7.F59936Im 2009   [E]—dc22   2008022458

ISBN 978-0-385-38654-8 (pbk.)

MANUFACTURED IN CHINA
10 9 8 7 6 5 4 3 2 1   First Dragonfly Books Edition 2014
Random House Children's Books supports the First Amendment
and celebrates the right to read.

IMOGENE'S LAST STAND

Written by
Candace Fleming

Illustrated by
Nancy Carpenter

Dragonfly Books ⟶ New York

Liddleville, New Hampshire, was small—so small it wasn't even a speck on the state map. Still, Liddleville was home to a village green, a general store, a three-legged cat, and a little girl named Imogene Tripp.

Imogene loved history.

When she was a baby, her first words were "Four score and seven years ago."

As a preschooler, she finger-painted an accurate map of the Oregon Trail.

And as a kindergartner, she used her show-and-tell time to give a series of lectures on important women in history.

next week: SojournerTruth

Now Imogene's attention was on the Liddleville Historical Society. The Society—a centuries-old house stuffed with dusty antiques—had sat at the end of Main Street unloved and unwanted until Imogene pushed open its creaky front door.

"Wow!"
she
exclaimed.

"What a mess," added her father.

Imogene shook her head. "This isn't a mess, Daddy," she declared. "This is history. And in the immortal words of Dr. Martin Luther King, Jr., '*We are made by history.*'"

Then she got busy sweeping away cobwebs, filing old letters, pasting yellowed photographs into albums, identifying fossils, organizing arrowheads, and even refinishing a four-poster bed.

When she was done, Imogene waited . . .

and waited . . .

and waited to give the townspeople a tour. But—

"In the immortal words of Davy Crockett," she sighed, "'Ain't nobody comin'.'"

Finally, one Monday morning, a workman arrived.
He pounded a sign into the Society's front yard.

NOTICE!
This house will be torn down
SATURDAY
so a shoelace factory can be
built in its place

By order of
Mayor I. M. Butz

CITY HAUL-AWAY

GRAND OPENING

Liddleville Historical Society

"Torn down?" cried Imogene. "But in the immortal words of William Morris, 'Old buildings do not belong to us; they belonged to our forefathers, and they will belong to our descendants.'"

The workman shrugged. "Tell it to the mayor."

So Imogene did.

When she finished, Mayor Butz shook his cheeks. "My position is firm. Out with the old, in with the new."

"What about the Society?" cried Imogene. "What about *history*?"

"Who cares about history?" snorted the mayor. "Shoelaces will put this town on the map." He showed her the door.

BUTZ

IFS ANDS BUTZ

DON'T BE A KLUTZ VOTE BUTZ

BUTZ

Tie one on in Liddleville

LIDDLEVILLE LACES

TIE THE KNOT IN LIDDLEVILLE

Out on the sidewalk, Imogene fumed. "I won't let it happen! In the immortal words of John Paul Jones, '*I have not yet begun to fight!*'"

And fight she did.

Tuesday morning, dressed in her Paul Revere costume from Halloween, Imogene galloped up and down Main Street. "The bulldozers are coming! The bulldozers are coming!" she shouted.

No one heeded her cry.

Finally, Mr. Tuttlewit stepped out of the general store. "Hold your ponies, little missy. Don't you know shoelaces are going to put this town on the map?"

Imogene snatched up her stick horse. "In the immortal words of Theodore Roosevelt, 'Balderdash!'"

She stomped home to her father.

But Wednesday morning she was at it again. Armed with stepladder and Scotch tape, she tied a red-white-and-blue ribbon around every tree, streetlight, stop sign, parking meter, mailbox, fire hydrant, bike rack, baby stroller, and dog collar in town.

"Don't let your past get smashed!" she cried.

No one joined her cause.

Finally, Officer Ditzwilliam said, "Those bows are real pretty, honey, but shoelaces will put this town on the map."

Imogene frowned.

She trudged home to her father.

But Thursday morning she was back. Up before dawn, she'd scribbled until her fingers cramped. Then, as the sun rose in the sky, a biplane dipped low over Liddleville and dropped hundreds of handmade flyers.

"Rally on the village green and save your history!" each one read.

No one rallied.

Finally, little Abner Pitt pedaled over on his tricycle. "Don'tcha understand, Immie? Shoelaces are gonna put this town on the map."
It was the last straw.

SAVE OUR HISTORY

Rally on the village green and Save your HISTORY!

"In the immortal words of Chief Joseph," she sobbed, "'*My heart is sick and sad.*'"
She ran home to her father.

All too soon it was Friday. Imogene wandered through her beloved Society.

"Goodbye, photographs," she sniffled. "Goodbye, fossils and four-poster bed. Goodbye, old letters."

A yellowed parchment caught her eye.

Imogene read it once.
She read it twice.
She read it aloud.

October 16, 1789

Dear Sir,

Thank you again for the hospitality you showed me last Tuesday. The oxtail soup was delicious and the four-poster bed soft as angel clouds. Indeed, I have not slept so well since leaving Mount Vernon.

Your humble and obedient servant—

G. Washington

Imogene gasped. George Washington? Had he really slept here?

Quickly, she wrote a message explaining everything to the renowned Liddleville historian, Professor Cornelia Pastmatters.

"Please hurry," Imogene begged. Then she clicked Send and began to pace. Time! If only she had more time! But how could she get some?

Inspiration struck.

And Imogene sprang into action.

When Saturday and the bulldozers
arrived, Imogene Tripp stood ready.

"In the immortal words of the Vietnam War protesters," she shouted,

"'*Heck no, I won't go!*'"

The bulldozers growled to a stop.

Watching . . . Waiting . . .

Her father came on the run.

"Imogene! Get out of the way!"

But Imogene squared her shoulders. "Daddy," she declared, "in the immortal words of Abraham Lincoln, '*A great oak is only a little nut that held its ground.*' I'm holding my ground."

Just then Mayor Butz huffed up the porch stairs. "Unlock yourself this instant!"

"Heck no, I won't go!" Imogene cried.

The mayor whirled on Imogene's father. "Do something."

Imogene's father looked from the mayor to his daughter and back again. "Heck no, we won't go!" he finally cried.

Mayor Butz's nostrils flared. "That pip-squeak can't stay on this porch forever. And when she moves? SMASH!" He stomped back to the bulldozers.

As the sun rose higher, the townsfolk gathered to see what was happening. Mr. Tuttlewit arrived. So did Officer Ditzwilliam. And little Abner Pitt. He called out, "Are you all right, Immie?"

"In the immortal words of President Martin Van Buren, *'I am OK,'*" she replied firmly.

By midafternoon, TV reporters had arrived. They rushed to interview the little girl who refused to leave the porch.

"In the immortal words of Eleanor Roosevelt, '*You must do the thing you think you cannot do*,'" Imogene told them.

Suddenly, a limousine appeared. Its door opened and out stepped—

"Professor Pastmatters!" gasped Imogene.

Followed by—

"The President of the United States!" gasped the crowd.

The President headed straight for the cameras. "I'm here to declare this house a national landmark." She held up a brass plaque. "George Washington slept here!"

Imogene whooped.

"We did it!"

"Yes indeed," agreed Professor Pastmatters.

"I'm so proud," said Imogene's father.

Little Abner Pitt stepped forward. "Wait!" he cried. "What about shoelaces?"

"Shoelaces?" Mayor Butz snorted. "Who cares about shoelaces?" He smiled for the cameras. "Why, our town's history will put us on the map."

The townspeople cheered.

The bulldozers rumbled away.

And Imogene plucked the key from her pocket and freed herself.

Then everyone—even Mayor Butz—went on a tour of the Liddleville Historical Society.

"In the immortal words of me," Imogene later said as she waved goodbye to the last of her guests, "*That was totally fun!*"

"It sure was," laughed her father. "It sure was."

IMOGENE TRIPP'S HISTORICAL TIDBITS

THEODORE "TEDDY" ROOSEVELT—When our twenty-sixth president liked something, he declared it "bully!" When he was angry or upset, he cried, "Balderdash!"

CHIEF JOSEPH—This leader of the Nez Percé Indians in the Pacific Northwest refused to let his people be forced onto a reservation in 1877, and tried to lead them over the Canadian border to freedom. Sadly, the United States Army caught them. The chief surrendered, saying, "Hear me, my chiefs. I am tired; my heart is sick and sad. From where the sun now stands, I will fight no more forever."

VIETNAM WAR PROTESTERS—Many citizens took a stand against the United States' military fight in North Vietnam, a country in Southeast Asia, between 1965 and 1975. At rallies, protesters would chant something very like "Heck no, we won't go!" Imogene had to change the quote a bit because she's not allowed to swear. What did she change? The word *heck*. What word did the protesters really use? We can't tell you, because we're not allowed to swear either.

ABRAHAM LINCOLN—When our sixteenth president was asked how he had managed to get that job after having failed at so many other things in his life, he answered, "It is like the old saying: 'A great oak is only a little nut that held its ground.'"

MARTIN VAN BUREN—Because he was born in Kinderhook, New York, our eighth president earned the nickname Old Kinderhook. At political rallies, Van Buren liked to cry, "I am Old Kinderhook and I am OK."

ELEANOR ROOSEVELT was a busy woman. Not only was she first lady of the United States from 1933 to 1945, but she was also a civil rights activist, a social reformer, a delegate to the United Nations General Assembly, and a writer. In her book *You Learn by Living*, she gave this advice: "You must do the thing you think you cannot do."

IMOGENE TRIPP will go down in history not just because she single-handedly saved her local historical society, but also because she uttered the immortal words, "That was totally fun!"